GRIMM'S FAIRY TALES

NINE STORIES

JACOB AND WILHELM GRIMM

GRIMM'S FAIRY TALES

NINE STORIES

penguin books

PENGUIN BOOKS
Published by the Penguin Group
Penguin Books USA Inc., 375 Hudson Street,
New York, New York 10014, U.S.A.
Penguin Books Ltd, 27 Wrights Lane,
London W8 5TZ, England
Penguin Books Australia Ltd, Ringwood, Victoria, Australia
Penguin Books Canada Ltd, 10 Alcorn Avenue,
Toronto, Ontario, Canada M4V 3B2
Penguin Books (N.Z.) Ltd, 182-190 Wairau Road,
Auckland 10, New Zealand

Penguin Books Ltd, Registered Offices:
Harmondsworth, Middlesex, England

Published in Penguin Books 1995

ISBN 0 14 60.0080 3

Printed in the United States of America

CONTENTS

The Frog Prince 1

The Twelve Dancing Princesses 7

The Mouse, the Bird, and the Sausage 13

The Goose Girl 16

Rapunzel 25

The Shoemaker and the Elves 31

Snow-White 34

The Six Swans 48

The Straw, the Coal, and the Bean 56

The Frog Prince

In the old times, when it was still of some use to wish for the thing one wanted, there lived a king whose daughters were all handsome, but the youngest was so beautiful that the sun himself, who has seen so much, wondered at her beauty each time he shone over her. Near the royal castle there was a great dark wood, and in the wood under an old linden tree was a well. When the day was hot, the King's daughter used to go forth into the wood and sit by the brink of the cool well. And if the time seemed long, she would take out a golden ball and throw it up and catch it again, and this was her favorite pastime.

Now it happened one day that the golden ball, instead of falling back into the maiden's little hand which had sent it aloft, dropped to the ground near the edge of the well and rolled in. The King's daughter followed it with her eyes as it sank, but the well was deep—so deep that the bottom could not be seen. Then she began to weep, and she wept and wept as if she could never be comforted.

And in the midst of her weeping she heard a voice saying to her, "What ails you, King's daughter? Your tears would melt a heart of stone."

And when she looked to see where the voice came from, there was nothing but a frog stretching his thick ugly head out of the water.

"Oh, is it you, old waddler?" said she. "I weep because my golden ball has fallen into the well."

"Never mind. Do not weep," said the frog. "I can help you. But what will you give me if I fetch up your ball?"

"Whatever you like, dear frog," said she. "Any of my clothes, my pearls and jewels, or even the golden crown that I wear."

"Your clothes, your pearls and jewels, and your golden crown are not for me," answered the frog. "But if you would love me, and have me for your companion and playfellow, and let me sit by you at table and eat from your plate and drink from your cup, and sleep in your little bed—if you would promise all this, then would I dive below the water and fetch you your golden ball again."

"Oh, yes," she answered, "I will promise it all, whatever you want, if you will only get me my ball again."

But she thought to herself, "What nonsense he talks! As if he could do anything but sit in the water and croak with the other frogs, or could possibly be anyone's companion!"

But the frog, as soon as he heard her promise, drew his head under the water and sank down out of sight. But after a while he came to the surface again with the ball in his mouth, and he threw it on the grass.

The King's daughter was overjoyed to see her pretty plaything again, and she caught it up and ran off with it.

"Stop, stop!" cried the frog. "Take me up too. I cannot run as fast as you!"

But it was of no use, for croak, croak after her as he might, she would not listen to him. Instead, she hastened home and very soon forgot all about the poor frog, who had to betake himself to his well again.

The next day, when the King's daughter was sitting at table with the King and all the court, and was eating from her golden plate, there came something pitter-patter up the marble stairs, and then there came a knocking at the door and a voice crying, "King's youngest daughter, let me in!"

And she got up and ran to see who it could be, but when she opened the door, there was the frog sitting outside. Then she shut the door hastily and went back to her seat, feeling very uneasy.

The King noticed how quickly her heart was beating and said, "My child, what are you afraid of? Is there a giant standing at the door ready to carry you away?"

"Oh no," answered she. "No giant, but a horrid frog."

"And what does the frog want?" asked the King.

"Oh, dear father," answered she, "when I was sitting by the well yesterday playing with my golden ball, it fell into the water. And while I was crying for the loss of it, the frog came and got it again for me on condition I would let him be my companion. I never thought that he could leave the water and come after me, but there he is now outside the door, and he wants to come in to me."

And then they all heard him knocking the second time and crying:

"King's youngest daughter,
Open to me!
By the well water
What promised you me?
King's youngest daughter,
Now open to me!"

"That which you have promised must you perform," said the King sternly. "So go now and let him in."

So she went and opened the door and the frog hopped in, following at her heels till she reached her chair.

Then he stopped and cried, "Lift me up to sit by you." But she delayed doing so until the King ordered her.

When once the frog was on the chair, he wanted to get on the table, and there he sat and said, "Now push your golden plate a little nearer so that we may eat together."

And so she did, but everybody could see how unwilling she was. And the frog feasted heartily, but every morsel seemed to stick in her throat.

 "I have had enough now," said the frog at last. "And as

I am tired, you must carry me to your room and make ready your silken bed, and we will lie down and go to sleep."

Then the King's daughter began to weep and was afraid of the cold frog, whom nothing would satisfy but he must sleep in her pretty clean bed.

Now the King grew angry with her and said, "What you have promised in your time of necessity, you must now perform."

So she picked up the frog with her finger and thumb, carried him upstairs, and put him in a corner. And when she had lain down to sleep, he came creeping up, saying, "I am tired and want sleep as much as you. Take me up or I will tell your father."

Then she felt beside herself with rage and, picking him up, she threw him with all her strength against the wall, crying, "Now will you be quiet, you horrid frog?"

But as he fell he ceased to be a frog, and became all at once a prince with beautiful kind eyes. And it came to pass that with her father's consent they became bride and bridegroom. And he told her how a wicked witch had bound him by her spells, and how no one but she alone could have released him, and that they two would go together to his father's kingdom.

And there came to the door a carriage drawn by eight white horses, with white plumes on their heads and with golden harness, and behind the carriage, faithful Henry, the servant of the young Prince, was standing. Now, faithful Henry had suffered such care and pain when his master was turned into a frog that he had been obliged to wear three iron bands over his heart, to keep it from breaking with trouble and anxiety. When the carriage started to take the Prince to his kingdom, and faithful Henry had helped them both in, he got up behind and was full of joy at his master's deliverance.

And when they had gone a part of the way, the Prince heard a sound at the back of the carriage as if something had broken, and he turned round and cried, "Henry, the wheel must be breaking!"

But Henry answered:

"The wheel does not break;
'Tis the band round my heart
That, to lessen its ache,
When I grieved for your sake,
I bound round my heart."

Again and yet once again there was the same sound, and the Prince thought it must be the wheel breaking, but it was the breaking of the other bands from faithful Henry's heart, because it was now so relieved and happy.

The Twelve Dancing Princesses

Once upon a time there was a king who had twelve daughters, each more beautiful than the other. They slept together in a hall where their beds stood close to one another. At night when they had gone to bed, the King locked the door and bolted it. When he unlocked it in the morning, he noticed that their shoes had been danced to pieces, and nobody could explain how it happened.

So the King sent out a proclamation saying that anyone who could discover where the princesses did their night's dancing might choose one of them to be his wife and should reign after his death. But whoever presented himself, and failed to make the discovery after three days and nights, was to forfeit his life.

A prince soon appeared and offered to take the risk. He was well received, and at night was taken into a room adjoining the hall where the princesses slept. His bed was made up there, and he was to watch and see where they went to dance. The door of the room was left open, so that they could not do anything or leave without being seen. But the prince's eyes grew heavy and he fell asleep. When he woke in the morning, all the princesses had been dancing, for the soles of their shoes were full of holes. The second and third evenings passed with the same results. The prince was then granted no mercy, and his head was cut off. Many others came after him and offered to take the risk, but they all forfeited their lives.

Now it happened that a poor soldier, who had been wounded and could no longer serve, found himself on the road to the town where the King lived. There he fell in with an old woman who asked him where he was going.

"I really don't know myself," he said. And he added in fun, "I should like to discover where the King's daughters dance their shoes into holes, and after that I should like to become king."

"That is not so difficult," said the old woman. "You must not drink the wine which will be brought to you in the evening, but must pretend to be fast asleep." Whereupon she gave him a short cloak, saying, "When you wear this you will be invisible, and then you can slip out after the twelve princesses."

When the soldier heard this good advice he considered it seriously, plucked up the courage to appear before the King, and offered himself as suitor. He was as well received as the others and was dressed in royal garments.

In the evening, when bedtime came, he was conducted to the anteroom. As he was about to go to bed the eldest princess appeared, bringing him a cup of wine. But he had fastened a sponge under his chin and let the wine run down into it, so that he did not drink one drop. Then he lay down, and when he had been quiet a little while he began to snore as though in the deepest sleep.

The twelve princesses heard him and laughed. The eldest said, "He too must forfeit his life."

Then they got up, opened cupboards, chests, and cases, and brought out their beautiful dresses. They decked themselves before the glass, skipping about and reveling in the prospect of the dance.

Only the youngest sister said, "I don't know what it is. You may rejoice, but I feel so strange. A misfortune is certainly hanging over us."

"You are a little goose," answered the eldest. "You are always frightened. Have you forgotten how many princes have come here in vain? Why, I need not have given the soldier a sleeping draught at all! The blockhead would never have awakened."

When they were all ready they looked at the soldier, but his eyes were shut and he did not stir. So they thought they would soon be quite safe. Then the eldest went up to one of the beds and knocked on it. It sank into the earth and they descended through the opening one after another, the eldest first.

The soldier, who had noticed everything, did not hesitate long, but threw on his cloak and went down behind the youngest. Halfway down he trod on her dress.

She was frightened and said, "What was that? Who is holding on to my dress?"

"Don't be so foolish. You must have caught it on a nail," said the eldest.

Then they went right down, and when they got quite underground they stood in a marvelously beautiful avenue of trees. All the leaves were silver, and glittered and shone.

The soldier thought, "I must take away some token with me." And as he broke off a twig, a sharp crack came from the tree.

The youngest cried out, "All is not well! Did you hear that sound?"

"Those are triumphal salutes because we have eluded our 'prince'!" said the eldest.

Next they came to an avenue where all the leaves were of gold, and at last into a third where they were of shining diamonds. From both these the soldier broke off a twig, and there was a crack each time which made the youngest princess start with terror. But the eldest maintained that the sounds were only triumphal salutes. They went faster and came to a great lake. Close to the bank lay twelve little boats and in every boat sat a handsome prince. They had expected the twelve princesses and each took one with him, but the soldier seated himself by the youngest.

Then said her prince, "I don't know why; but the boat

is much heavier today. I am obliged to row with all my strength to get it along."

"I wonder why it is," said the youngest, "unless perhaps it is the hot weather. It is strangely hot."

On the opposite side of the lake stood a splendid brightly lighted castle from which came the sound of the joyous music of trumpets and drums. They rowed across, and every prince danced with his love. And the soldier danced too, unseen. If one of the princesses held a cup of wine he drank out of it, so that it was empty when she lifted it to her lips. This frightened the youngest one, but the eldest always silenced her.

They danced till three next morning, when their shoes were danced into holes and they were obliged to stop. The princes took them back across the lake, and this time the soldier took his seat beside the eldest. On the bank they said farewell to their princes and promised to come again the next night.

When they got to the steps the soldier ran on ahead, lay down in bed, and when the twelve came lagging by, slowly and wearily, he began to snore again very loud, so that they said, "We are quite safe so far as he is concerned." Then they took off their beautiful dresses, put them away, placed the worn-out shoes under their beds, and lay down.

The next morning the soldier determined to say nothing, but to see the wonderful doings again. So he went with them the second and third nights. Everything was just the same as the first time, and they danced each time till their shoes were in holes. The third time the soldier took away a wine cup as a token.

When the appointed hour came for his answer, he took the three twigs and the cup with him and went before the King. The twelve princesses stood behind the door listening to hear what he would say.

When the King put the question, "Where did my daughters dance their shoes to pieces in the night?" he answered, "With twelve princes in an underground castle." Then he produced the tokens.

The King sent for his daughters and asked them whether the soldier had spoken the truth. As they saw they were betrayed and would gain nothing by lies, they were obliged to admit all.

Thereupon the King asked the soldier which one he would choose as his wife. He answered, "I am no longer young. Give me the eldest."

So the wedding was celebrated that very day, and the kingdom was promised to him on the King's death. But for every night which the underground princes had spent in dancing with the princesses, a day was added to their time of enchantment.

The Mouse, the Bird, and the Sausage

Once upon a time a mouse and a bird and a sausage lived and kept house together in perfect peace among themselves, and in great prosperity. It was the bird's business to fly to the forest every day and bring back wood. The mouse had to draw the water, make the fire, and set the table. And the sausage had to do the cooking. Nobody is content in this world: much will have more. One day the bird met another bird on the way, and told him of his excellent condition in life. But the other bird called him a poor simpleton to do so much work while the two others led easy lives at home.

When the mouse had made up her fire and drawn water, she went to rest in her little room until it was time to lay the cloth. The sausage stayed by the saucepans, looked to it that the victuals were well cooked, and just before dinnertime he stirred the broth or the stew three or four times well around himself, so as to enrich and season and flavor it. Then the bird used to come home and lay down his load, and they sat down to table; and after a good meal they would go to bed and sleep their fill till the next morning. It really was a most satisfactory life.

But the bird came to the resolution next day never again to fetch wood. He had, he said, been their slave long enough. Now they must change about and make a new arrangement. So in spite of all the mouse and the sausage could say, the bird was determined to have his own way. So they drew lots to settle it, and as the lot fell, the sausage was to fetch wood, the mouse was to cook, and the bird was to draw water and make the fire.

Now see what happened. The sausage went away after wood, the bird made up the fire, and the mouse put on the pot, and they waited until the sausage should come home, bringing the wood for the next day. But the sausage was absent so long that they thought something must have happened to him, and the bird went part of the way to see if he could see anything of him. Not far off he met a dog on the road, who, looking upon the sausage as lawful prey, had picked him up and made an end of him. The bird then lodged a complaint against the dog as an open and flagrant robber, but it was all no good, as the dog declared that he had found forged letters upon the sausage, so that he deserved to lose his life.

The bird then very sadly took up the wood and carried it home himself, and related to the mouse all he had seen and heard. They were both very troubled, but determined to look on the bright side of things and still to remain together. And so the bird laid the cloth, and the mouse prepared the food and finally got into the pot, as the sausage used to do, to stir and flavor the broth, but then she had to part with fur and skin and finally with life!

And when the bird came to dish up the dinner, there was no cook to be seen. And he turned over the heap of wood, and looked and looked, but the cook never appeared again. By accident the wood caught fire, and the bird hastened to fetch water to put it out, but he let fall the bucket in the well and himself after it, and as he could not get out again he was obliged to be drowned.

The Goose Girl

There was once an old queen whose husband had been dead for many years, and she had a very beautiful daughter. When she grew up she was betrothed to a prince in a distant country. When the time came for the maiden to be sent into this distant country to be married, the old Queen packed up quantities of clothes and jewels, gold and silver, cups and ornaments, and in fact everything suitable to a royal outfit, for she loved her daughter very dearly.

She also sent a waiting-woman to travel with her and to put her hand into that of the bridegroom. They each had a horse. The Princess' horse was called Falada, and it could speak.

When the hour of departure came, the old Queen went to her bedroom and with a sharp little knife cut her finger and made it bleed. Then she held a piece of white cambric under it and let three drops of blood fall on it. This cambric she gave to her daughter and said, "Dear child, take good care of this. It will stand you in good stead on the journey."

 They then bade each other a sorrowful farewell. The

Princess hid the piece of cambric in her bosom, mounted her horse, and set out to her bridegroom's country.

When they had ridden for a time, the Princess became very thirsty and said to the waiting-woman, "Get down and fetch me some water in my cup from the stream. I must have something to drink."

"If you are thirsty," said the waiting-woman, "dismount yourself, lie down by the water, and drink. I don't choose to be your servant."

So in her great thirst the Princess dismounted and stooped down to the stream and drank, since she could not have her golden cup. The poor Princess said, "Alas!" And the drops of blood answered, "If your mother knew this it would break her heart."

The royal bride was humble, so she said nothing, but mounted her horse again. Then they rode several miles further, but the day was warm, the sun was scorching, and the Princess was soon very thirsty again.

When they reached a river she called out again to her waiting-woman, "Get down and give me some water in my golden cup." She had forgotten all about the rude words which had been said to her.

But the waiting-woman answered more haughtily than ever, "If you want to drink, get the water for yourself. I won't be your servant."

Being very thirsty, the Princess dismounted and knelt by the flowing water. She cried, "Ah me!" And the drops of blood answered, "If your mother knew this it would break her heart."

While she stooped over the water to drink, the piece of cambric with the drops of blood on it fell out of her bosom and floated away on the stream, but she never noticed this in her great fear. The waiting-woman, however, had seen it and rejoiced at getting more power over the bride, who by losing the drops of blood had become weak and powerless.

Now when she was about to mount her horse Falada again, the waiting-woman said, "By rights, Falada belongs to me. This jade will do for you!"

The poor little Princess was obliged to give way. Then the waiting-woman in a harsh voice ordered her to take off her royal robes, and to put on her own mean garments. Finally she forced her to swear before heaven that she would not tell a creature at the court what had taken place. Had she not taken the oath she would have been killed on the spot. But Falada saw all this and marked it.

The waiting-woman mounted Falada and put the real bride on her poor jade, and they continued their journey.

There was great rejoicing when they arrived at the castle. The Prince hurried towards them and lifted the waiting-woman from her horse, thinking that she was his bride. She was led upstairs, but the real Princess had to stay below.

 The old King looked out of the window and saw the

delicate, pretty little creature standing in the courtyard. So he went to the bridal apartment and asked the bride about her companion who was left standing in the courtyard, and wished to know who she was.

"I picked her up on the way and brought her with me for company. Give the girl something to do to keep her from idling."

But the old King had no work for her and could not think of anything. At last he said, "I have a little lad who looks after the geese. She may help him."

The boy was called little Conrad, and the real bride was sent with him to look after the geese.

Soon afterwards, the false bride said to the Prince, "Dear husband, I pray you do me a favor."

He answered, "That will I gladly do."

"Well then, let the knacker be called to cut off the head of the horse I rode. It angered me on the way."

Really she was afraid that the horse would speak and tell of her treatment of the Princess. So it was settled, and the faithful Falada had to die.

When this came to the ear of the real Princess, she promised the knacker a piece of gold if he would do her a slight service. There was a great dark gateway to the town, through which she had to pass every morning and evening. Would he nail up Falada's head in this gateway so that she might see him as she passed?

The knacker promised to do as she wished, and when

the horse's head was cut off he hung it up in the dark gateway. In the early morning, when she and Conrad went through the gateway, she said in passing:

"Alas! dear Falada, there thou hangest."

And the head answered:

"Alas! Queen's daughter, there thou gangest.
If thy mother knew thy fate,
Her heart would break with grief so great."

Then they passed on out of the town and right into the fields with the geese. When they reached the meadow, the Princess sat down on the grass and let down her hair. It shone like pure gold, and when little Conrad saw it he was so delighted that he wanted to pluck some out. But she said:

"Blow, blow, little breeze,
And Conrad's hat seize.
Let him join in the chase
While away it is whirled,
Till my tresses are curled
And I rest in my place."

Then a strong wind sprang up which blew away Conrad's hat right over the fields, and he had to run after it. When he came back, she had finished combing her hair and it was all put up again, so he could not get a single hair. This made him very sulky and he would not say another word to her. And they tended the geese till evening, when they went home.

Next morning when they passed under the gateway, the Princess said:

"Alas! dear Falada, there thou hangest."

Falada answered:

"Alas! Queen's daughter, there thou gangest.
If thy mother knew thy fate,
Her heart would break with grief so great."

Again when they reached the meadows, the Princess undid her hair and began combing it. Conrad ran to pluck some out, but she said quickly:

"Blow, blow, little breeze,
And Conrad's hat seize.
Let him join in the chase
While away it is whirled,
Till my tresses are curled
And I rest in my place."

The wind again sprang up and blew Conrad's hat far away over the fields, and he had to run after it. When he came back, the hair was all put up again and he could not pull out a single hair. And they tended the geese till the evening.

When they got home Conrad went to the old King and said, "I won't tend the geese with that maiden again."

"Why not?" asked the King.

"Oh, she vexes me every day."

The old King then ordered him to tell what she did to vex him.

Conrad said, "In the morning when we pass under the dark gateway with the geese, she talks to a horse's head which is hung up on the wall. She says:

Alas! Falada, there thou hangest.

And the head answers:

Alas! Queen's daughter, there thou gangest.
If thy mother knew thy fate,
Her heart would break with grief so great."

Then Conrad went on to tell the King all that had happened in the meadow, and how he had to run after his hat in the wind.

The old King ordered Conrad to go out the next day as usual. Then he placed himself behind the dark gateway and heard the Princess speaking to Falada's head. He also followed her into the field and hid himself behind a bush. And with his own eyes he saw the Goose Girl and the lad come driving the geese into the field. Then after a time he saw the girl let down her hair, which glittered in the sun. Directly after this, she said:

"Blow, blow, little breeze,
And Conrad's hat seize.
Let him join in the chase
While away it is whirled,
Till my tresses are curled
And I rest in my place."

Then came a puff of wind which carried off Conrad's hat, and he had to run after it. While he was away, the maiden combed and did up her hair, and all this the old King observed. Thereupon he went away unnoticed, and in the evening when the Goose Girl came home, he called her aside and asked why she did all these things.

"I may not tell you that, nor may I tell any human creature, for I have sworn it under the open sky. If I had not done so, I should have lost my life."

He pressed her sorely and gave her no peace, but he could get nothing out of her. Then he said, "If you won't tell me, then tell your sorrows to the iron stove there." And he went away.

She crept up to the stove and, beginning to weep and lament, unburdened her heart to it and said, "Here I am, forsaken by all the world, and yet I am a princess. A false waiting-woman brought me to such a pass that I had to take off my royal robes. The she took my place with my bridegroom, while I have to do mean service as a goose girl. If my mother knew it, it would break her heart."

The old King stood outside by the pipes of the stove

and heard all that she said. Then he came back and told her to go away from the stove. He caused royal robes to be put upon her, and her beauty was a marvel. The old King called his son and told him that he had a false bride—she was only a waiting-woman, but the true bride was here, the so-called Goose Girl.

The young Prince was charmed with her youth and beauty. A great banquet was prepared to which all the courtiers and good friends were bidden. The bridegroom sat at the head of the table with the Princess on one side and the waiting-woman at the other, but she was dazzled and did not recognize the Princess in her brilliant apparel.

When they had eaten and drunk and were all very merry, the old King put a riddle to the waiting-woman. "What does a person deserve who deceives his master?" Then he told the whole story and ended by asking, "What doom does he deserve?"

The false bride answered, "No better than this: he must be put stark naked into a barrel stuck with nails, and be dragged along by two white horses from street to street till he is dead."

"That is your own doom!" said the King, "and the judgment shall be carried out."

When the sentence was fulfilled, the young Prince married his true bride, and they ruled their kingdom together in peace and happiness.

Rapunzel

There was once a man and his wife who had long wished in vain for a child, and at last they had reason to hope that heaven would grant their wish. There was a little window at the back of their house, which overlooked a beautiful garden full of lovely flowers and shrubs. It was, however, surrounded by a high wall, and nobody dared to enter it, because it belonged to a powerful witch who was feared by everybody.

One day the woman, standing at this window and looking into the garden, saw a bed planted with beautiful rampion. It looked so fresh and green that she longed to eat some of it. This longing increased every day; and as she knew it could never be satisfied, she began to look pale and miserable and to pine away. Then her husband was alarmed and said, "What ails you, my dear wife?"

"Alas!" she answered. "If I cannot get any of the rampion to eat from the garden behind our house, I shall die."

Her husband, who loved her, thought, "Before you let your wife die you must fetch her some of that rampion, cost what it may." So in the twilight he climbed over the wall into the witch's garden, hastily picked a handful of rampion, and took it back to his wife. She immediately prepared it and ate it very eagerly. It was so very, very nice that the next day her longing for it increased threefold. She could have no peace unless her husband fetched her some more. So in the twilight he set out again, but when he got over the wall he was terrified to see the witch before him.

"How dare you come into my garden like a thief and steal my rampion?" she said, with angry looks. "It shall be the worse for you!"

"Alas!" he answered. "Be merciful to me. I am only here from necessity. My wife sees your rampion from the window, and she has such a longing for it that she would die if she could not get some of it."

The anger of the witch abated and she said to him, "If it is as you say, I will allow you to take away with you as much rampion as you like, but on one condition. You must give me the child which your wife is about to bring into the world. I will care for it like a mother, and all will be well with it."

In his fear the man consented to everything. And when the baby was born, the witch appeared, gave it the name of Rapunzel (rampion), and took it away with her.

Rapunzel was the most beautiful child under the sun. When she was twelve years old, the witch shut her up in
 a tower which stood in a wood. It had neither staircase

nor doors, but only a little window quite high up in the wall.

When the witch wanted to enter the tower, she stood at the foot of it and cried:

"Rapunzel, Rapunzel, let down your hair!" Rapunzel had splendid long hair, as fine as spun gold. As soon as she heard the voice of the witch, she unfastened her plaits and twisted them round a hook by the window. They fell twenty ells downwards, and the witch climbed up by them.

It happened a couple of years later that the King's son rode through the forest and came close to the tower. From thence he heard a song so lovely that he stopped to listen. It was Rapunzel who in her loneliness made her sweet voice resound to pass away the time. The King's son wanted to join her, and he sought for the door of the tower but there was none to find.

He rode home, but the song had touched his heart so deeply that he went into the forest every day to listen to it. Once when he was hidden behind a tree he saw a witch come to the tower and call out:

"Rapunzel, Rapunzel, let down your hair!"

Then Rapunzel lowered her plaits of hair and the witch climbed up to her.

"If that is the ladder by which one ascends," he thought, "I will try my luck myself." And the next day, when it began to grow dark, he went to the tower and cried:

"Rapunzel, Rapunzel, let down your hair!"

The hair fell down and the King's son climbed up it.

At first Rapunzel was terrified, for she had never set eyes on a man before. But the King's son talked to her kindly, and told her that his heart had been so deeply touched by her song that he had no peace and was obliged to see her. Then Rapunzel lost her fear. And when he asked if she would have him for her husband, and she saw that he was young and handsome, she thought, "He will love me better than old Mother Gothel." So she said, "Yes," and laid her hand in his. She said, "I will gladly go with you, but I do not know how I am to get down from this tower. When you come, will you bring a skein of silk with you every time? I will twist it into a ladder, and when it is long enough I will descend by it, and you can take me away with you on your horse."

She arranged with him that he should come and see her every evening, for the old witch came in the daytime. The witch discovered nothing till suddenly Rapunzel said to her, "Tell me, Mother Gothel, how can it be that you are so much heavier to draw up than the young prince who will be here before long?"

"Oh, you wicked child, what do you say? I thought I had separated you from all the world, and yet you have deceived me." In her rage she seized Rapunzel's beautiful hair, twisted it twice round her left hand, snatched up a pair of shears, and cut off the plaits, which fell to the ground. She was so merciless that she took poor Rapunzel away into a wilderness, where she forced her to live in the greatest grief and misery.

In the evening of the day on which she had banished Rapunzel, the witch fastened the plaits which she had cut off to the hook by the window. And when the Prince came and called: "Rapunzel, Rapunzel, let down your hair!" she lowered the hair. The Prince climbed up, but there he found, not his beloved Rapunzel, but the witch, who looked at him with angry and wicked eyes.

"Ah!" she cried mockingly, "you have come to fetch your ladylove, but the pretty bird is no longer in her nest. And she can sing no more, for the cat has seized her and it will scratch your own eyes out too. Rapunzel is lost to you. You will never see her again."

The Prince was beside himself with grief, and in his despair he sprang out of the window. He was not killed, but his eyes were scratched out by the thorns among which he fell. He wandered about blind in the wood and had nothing but roots and berries to eat. He did nothing but weep and lament over the loss of his beloved wife Rapunzel. In this way he wandered about for some years, till at last he reached the wilderness where Rapunzel had been living in great poverty. He heard a voice which seemed very familiar to him and he went towards it.

Rapunzel knew him at once and fell weeping upon his neck. Two of her tears fell upon his eyes, and they immediately grew quite clear and he could see as well as ever.

He took her to his kingdom, where he was received with joy, and they lived long and happily together.

The Shoemaker and the Elves

There was once a shoemaker who through no fault of his own had become so poor that at last he had only leather enough left for one pair of shoes. At evening he cut out the shoes which he intended to begin upon the next morning, and since he had a good conscience, he lay down quietly, said his prayers, and fell asleep.

In the morning, when he had said his prayers and was preparing to sit down to work, he found the pair of shoes standing finished on his table. He was amazed and could not understand it in the least.

He took the shoes in his hand to examine them more closely. They were so neatly sewn that not a stitch was out of place, and were as good as the work of a master hand.

Soon afterwards a purchaser came in and, as he was much pleased with the shoes, he paid more than the ordinary price for them, so that the shoemaker was able to buy leather for two pairs of shoes with the money.

He cut them out in the evening, and the next day with fresh courage was about to go to work. But he had no need to, for when he got up the shoes were finished, and buyers were not lacking. These gave him so much money that he was able to buy leather for four pairs of shoes.

Early next morning he found the four pairs finished, and so it went on. What he cut out at evening was finished in the morning, so that he was soon again in comfortable circumstances and became a well-to-do man.

Now it happened one evening not long before Christmas, when he had cut out some shoes as usual, that he said to his wife, "How would it be if we were to sit up tonight to see who it is that lends us such a helping hand?"

The wife agreed and lighted a candle, and they hid themselves in the corner of the room behind the clothes which were hanging there. At midnight came two little naked men who sat down at the shoemaker's table, took up the cut-out work, and began with their tiny fingers to stitch, sew, and hammer so neatly and quickly that the shoemaker could not believe his eyes. They did not stop till everything was quite finished and stood complete on the table. Then they ran swiftly away.

The next day the wife said, "The little men have made us rich, and we ought to show our gratitude. They were running about with nothing on, and must freeze with cold. Now I will make them little shirts, coats, waistcoats, and hose, and will even knit them a pair of stockings. And you shall make them each a pair of shoes."

The husband agreed. And at evening, when they had everything ready, they laid out the presents on the table and hid themselves to see how the little men would behave.

At midnight they came skipping in and were about to set to work. But instead of the leather ready cut out, they found the charming little clothes.

At first they were surprised, then excessively delighted. With the greatest speed they put on and smoothed down the pretty clothes, singing:

"Now we're boys so fine and neat,
Why cobble more for others' feet?"

Then they hopped and danced about, and leapt over chairs and tables and out the door. Henceforward they came back no more, but the shoemaker fared well as long as he lived, and had good luck in all his undertakings.

Snow-White

Once upon a time in the middle of winter, when the snowflakes were falling like feathers from the sky, a queen sat at her window working, and her embroidery frame was of ebony. And as she worked, gazing at times out on the snow, she pricked her finger, and there fell from it three drops of blood on the snow. And when she saw how bright and red it looked, she said to herself, "Oh, that I had a child as white as snow, as red as blood, and as black as the wood of the embroidery frame!"

Not very long afterwards she had a daughter, with skin as white as snow, lips as red as blood, and hair as black as ebony, and she was named Snow-White. And when she was born the Queen died.

After a year had gone by, the King took another wife, a beautiful woman, but proud and overbearing, and she could not bear to be surpassed in beauty by anyone. She had a magic looking glass, and she used to stand before it and look in it and say:

"Looking glass upon the wall,
Who is fairest of us all?"

And the looking glass would answer:

"You are fairest of them all."

And she was contented, for she knew that the looking glass spoke the truth.

Now Snow-White was growing prettier and prettier, and when she was seven years old she was as beautiful as day, far more so than the Queen herself. So one day when the Queen went to her mirror and said:

"Looking glass upon the wall,
Who is fairest of us all?"

It answered:

"Queen, you are full fair, 'tis true,
But Snow-White fairer is than you."

This gave the Queen a great shock, and she became yellow and green with envy, and from that hour her heart turned against Snow-White and she hated her. And envy and pride like ill weeds grew higher in her heart every day until she had no peace day or night.

At last she sent for a huntsman and said, "Take the child out into the woods, so that I may set eyes on her no more. You must put her to death and bring me her heart for a token."

The huntsman consented and led her away. But when he drew his cutlass to pierce Snow-White's innocent heart, she began to weep and to say, "Oh, dear huntsman, do not take my life. I will go away into the wildwood and never come home again."

And as she was so lovely the huntsman had pity on her and said, "Away with you then, poor child."

He thought the wild animals would be sure to devour her, and it was as if a stone had been rolled away from his heart when he was spared putting her to death.

Just at that moment a young wild boar came running by, so he caught and killed it. And taking out its heart, he brought it to the Queen for a token. And it was salted and cooked and the wicked woman ate it up, thinking that there was an end of Snow-White.

Now when the poor child found herself quite alone in the wild woods, she felt full of terror, even of the very leaves on the trees, and she did not know what to do for fright. Then she began to run over the sharp stones and through the thorn bushes, and the wild beasts ran about her but they did her no harm. She ran as long as her feet would carry her. And when the evening drew near she came to a little house and she went inside to rest. Everything there was very small, but as pretty and clean as possible. There stood a little table, ready laid. It was covered with a white cloth and seven little plates, and seven knives and forks, and drinking cups. By the wall stood seven little beds side by side, covered with clean white quilts.

Snow-White, being very hungry and thirsty, ate from

each plate a little porridge and bread, and drank out of each little cup a drop of wine, so as not to finish up any one portion. After that she felt so tired that she lay down in turn on each of the beds, but none of them seemed to suit her. One was too long, another too short; but at last the seventh was quite right, and so she lay down upon it, committed herself to heaven, and fell asleep.

When it was quite dark, the masters of the house came home. They were seven dwarfs whose work it was to dig underground among the mountains. When they had lighted their seven candles and it was quite light in the little house, they saw that someone must have been in, as everything was not in the same order in which they left it.

The first said, "Who has been sitting in my little chair?"

The second said, "Who has been eating from my little plate?"

The third said, "Who has been taking from my little loaf?"

The fourth said, "Who has been tasting my porridge?"

The fifth said, "Who has been using my little fork?"

The sixth said, "Who has been cutting with my little knife?"

The seventh said, "Who has been drinking from my little cup?"

Then the first one, looking round, saw a hollow in his bed and cried, "Who has been lying on my bed?"

And the others came running and cried, "Someone has been on our beds too!"

But when the seventh looked at his bed, he saw little Snow-White lying there asleep. Then he told the others, who came running up, crying out in their astonishment and holding up their seven little candles to throw a light upon Snow-White.

"Goodness gracious!" they cried. "What beautiful child is this?" And they were so full of joy to see her that they did not wake her, but let her sleep on. And the seventh dwarf slept with his comrades, an hour at a time with each, until the night had passed.

When it was morning, and Snow-White awoke and saw the seven dwarfs, she was very frightened. But they seemed quite friendly and asked her what her name was, and she told them. Then they asked her how she came to be in their house. And she related to them how her step-mother had wished her to be put to death, and how the huntsman had spared her life, and how she had run the whole day long until at last she had found their little house.

Then the dwarfs said, "If you will keep our house for us, and cook, and wash, and make the beds, and sew and knit, and keep everything tidy and clean, you may stay with us, and you shall lack nothing."

"With all my heart," said Snow-White. And so she stayed and kept the house in good order. In the morning the dwarfs went to the mountain to dig for gold. In the evening they came home, and their supper had to be ready for them.

All the day long the maiden was left alone, and the good little dwarfs warned her, saying, "Beware of your stepmother! She will soon know you are here. Let no one into the house."

Now the Queen, having eaten Snow-White's heart, as she supposed, felt quite sure that now she was the first and fairest, and so she came to her mirror and said:

"Looking glass upon the wall,
Who is fairest of us all?"

And the glass answered:

"Queen, thou art of beauty rare,
But Snow-White living in the glen
With the seven little men
Is a thousand times more fair."

Then she was very angry, for the glass always spoke the truth, and she knew that the huntsman must have deceived her and that Snow-White must still be living. And she thought and thought how she could manage to make an end of her, for as long as she was not the fairest in the land, envy left her no rest. At last she thought of a plan. She painted her face and dressed herself like an old peddler woman, so that no one would have known her. In this disguise she went across the seven mountains, until she came to the house of the seven little dwarfs.

And she knocked at the door and cried, "Fine wares to sell! Fine wares to sell!"

Snow-White peeped out of the window and cried, "Good day, good woman, what have you to sell?"

"Good wares, fine wares," answered she. "Laces of all colors." And she held up a piece that was woven of many–colored silk.

"I need not be afraid of letting in this good woman," thought Snow-White, and she unbarred the door and bought the pretty lace.

"What a figure you are child!" said the old woman. "Come and let me lace your bodice properly for once."

Snow-White, suspecting nothing, stood up before her and let her lace her with the new lace. But the old woman laced so quickly and tightly that it took Snow-White's breath away, and she fell down as dead.

"Now you are no longer the fairest," said the old woman as she hastened away.

Not long after that, towards evening, the seven dwarfs came home, and they were terrified to see their dear Snow-White lying on the ground without life or motion. They raised her up, and when they saw how tightly the lace was drawn, they cut it in two. Then she began to draw breath, and little by little she returned to life.

 When the dwarfs heard what had happened they said,

"The old peddler woman was no other than the wicked Queen. You must beware of letting anyone in when we are not here!"

And when the wicked woman got home she went to her glass and said:

"Looking glass against the wall,
Who is fairest of us all?"

And it answered as before:

"Queen, thou art of beauty rare,
But Snow-White living in the glen
With the seven little men
Is a thousand times more fair."

When she heard that, she was so struck with surprise that all the blood left her heart, for she knew that Snow-White must still be living.

"But now," said she, "I will think of something that will be her ruin." And by witchcraft she made a poisoned comb. Then she dressed herself up to look like another and different sort of old woman.

So she went across the seven mountains and came to the house of the seven dwarfs, and knocked at the door and cried, "Good wares to sell! good wares to sell!"

Snow-White looked out and said, "Go away, I must not let anybody in."

"But you are not forbidden to look," said the old woman, taking out the poisoned comb and holding it up. It pleased the poor child so much that she was tempted to open the door. And when the bargain was made the old woman said, "Now for once your hair shall be properly combed."

Poor Snow-White, thinking no harm, let the old woman do as she would, but no sooner was the comb put in her hair than the poison began to work, and the poor girl fell down senseless.

"Now, you paragon of beauty," said the wicked woman, "this is the end of you!" And she went off.

By good luck it was now near evening and the seven little dwarfs came home. When they saw Snow-White lying on the ground as dead, they thought directly that it was the stepmother's doing. They looked about and found the poisoned comb, and no sooner had they drawn it out of her hair than Snow-White came to herself and related all that had passed. Then they warned her once more to be on her guard, and never again to let anyone in at the door.

And the Queen went home and stood before the looking glass and said:

"Looking glass against the wall,
Who is fairest of us all?"

 And the looking glass answered as before:

"Queen, thou art of beauty rare,
But Snow-White living in the glen
With the seven little men
Is a thousand times more fair."

When she heard the looking glass speak thus she trembled and shook with anger.

"Snow-White shall die," cried she, "though it should cost me my own life!"

And then she went to a secret lonely chamber where no one was likely to come, and there she made a poisonous apple. It was beautiful to look upon, being white with red cheeks, so that anyone who should see it must long for it, but whoever ate even a little bit of it must die. When the apple was ready, she painted her face and clothed herself like a peasant woman, and went across the seven mountains to where the seven dwarfs lived.

And when she knocked at the door Snow-White put her head out of the window and said, "I dare not let anybody in. The seven dwarfs told me not to."

"All right," answered the woman. "I can easily get rid of my apples elsewhere. There, I will give you one."

"No," answered Snow-White. "I dare not take it."

"Are you afraid of poison?" said the woman. "Look here, I will cut the apple in two pieces. You shall have the red side. I will have the white one."

The apple was so cunningly made that all of the poison

was in the rosy half of it. Snow-White longed for the beautiful apple. And as she saw the peasant woman eating a piece of it she could no longer refrain, but stretched out her hand and took the poisoned half. But no sooner had she taken a morsel of it into her mouth than she fell to the earth as dead.

And the Queen, casting on her a terrible glance, laughed aloud and cried, "As white as snow, as red as blood, as black as ebony! This time the dwarfs will not be able to bring you to life again."

When she went home and asked the looking glass:

"Looking glass against the wall,
Who is fairest of us all?"

—at last it answered, "You are the fairest now of all."

Then her envious heart had peace, as much as an envious heart can have.

The dwarfs, when they came home in the evening, found Snow-White lying on the ground, and there came no breath out of her mouth, and she was dead. They lifted her up, sought if anything poisonous was to be found, cut her laces, combed her hair, washed her with water and wine, but all was of no avail. The poor child was dead, and remained dead. Then they laid her on a bier, and all seven of them sat around it, and wept and lamented three whole days. And then they would have buried her, except that she still looked as if she were living, with her beautiful blooming cheeks. So they said, "We cannot hide her away in the black ground."

And they had made a coffin of clear glass, that could be looked into from all sides. They laid her in it and wrote upon it in golden letters her name, and that she was a king's daughter. Then they set the coffin out upon the mountain and one of them always remained by it to watch. And the birds came too and mourned for Snow-White: first an owl, then a raven, and last, a dove.

Now for a long while Snow-White lay in the coffin and never changed, but looked as if she were asleep, for she was still as white as snow, as red as blood, and her hair was as black as ebony. It happened, however, that one day a king's son rode through the wood and up to the dwarfs' house, which was near it. He saw on the mountain the coffin, and beautiful Snow-White within it, and he read what was written in golden letters upon it.

Then he said to the dwarfs, "Let me have the coffin, and I will give you whatever you like to ask for it."

But the dwarfs told him that they could not part with it for all the gold in the world.

But he said, "I beseech you to give it to me, for I cannot live without looking upon Snow-White. If you consent, I will bring you to great honor and care for you as if you were my brethren."

When he pleaded, the good little dwarfs had pity upon

him and gave him the coffin, and the King's son called his servants and bid them carry it away on their shoulders. Now it happened that as they were going along they stumbled over a bush, and with the shaking the bit of poisoned apple flew out of her throat. It was not long before she opened her eyes, threw up the cover of the coffin, and sat up, alive and well. "Oh dear, where am I?" cried she.

The King's son answered, full of joy, "You are near me." And relating all that had happened, he said, "I would rather have you than anything in the world. Come with me to my father's castle and you shall be my bride."

And Snow-White was kind and went with him, and their wedding was held with pomp and great splendor.

But Snow-White's wicked stepmother was also bidden to the feast. And when she had dressed herself in beautiful clothes she went to her looking glass and said:

"Looking glass upon the wall,
Who is fairest of us all?"

The looking glass answered:

"O Queen, although you are of beauty rare,
The young bride is a thousand times more fair."

Then she railed and cursed, and was beside herself with disappointment and anger. First she thought she would not go to the wedding, but then she felt she should have no peace until she went and saw the bride. And when she saw her she knew her for Snow-White, and could not stir from the place for anger and terror. For they had ready red-hot iron shoes, in which she had to dance until she fell down dead.

The Six Swans

Once upon a time a king was hunting in a great wood, and he pursued a wild animal so eagerly that none of his people could follow him. When evening came he stood still; then looking round him he found that he had lost his way, and seeking a path, he found none. Then all at once he saw an old woman with a nodding head coming up to him, and she was a witch.

"My good woman," said he, "can you show me the way out of the wood?"

"Oh yes, my Lord King," answered she. "Certainly I can, but I must make a condition. And if you do not fulfill it, you will never get out of the wood again, but will die there of hunger."

"What is the condition?" asked the King.

"I have a daughter," said the old woman, "who is as fair as any in the world. If you will take her for your bride and make her your Queen, I will show you the way out of the wood."

The King consented because of the difficulty he was in, and the old woman led him into her little house, where her daughter was sitting by the fire.

She received the King just as if she had been expecting him. And though he saw that she was very beautiful, she did not please him, and he could not look at her without an inward shudder. Nevertheless he took the maiden before him on his horse, and the old woman showed him the way, and soon he was in his royal castle again, where the wedding was held.

The King had been married before and his first wife had left seven children, six boys and one girl, whom he loved better than all the world. And as he was afraid the stepmother might not behave well to them, and perhaps would do them some mischief, he took them to a lonely castle standing in the middle of a wood.

There they remained hidden, for the road to it was so hard to find that the King himself could not have found it had it not been for a ball of yarn with wonderful properties, which a wise woman had given him. When he threw this down before him, it unrolled itself and showed him the way.

But the King went so often to see his dear children that the Queen was displeased at his absence. She became curious and wanted to know why he went out alone in the wood so often. She bribed his servants with much money, and they showed her the secret and told her of the ball of yarn, which alone could point out the way. Then she gave herself no rest until she had found out where the King kept the ball. Then she made some little white silk shirts and sewed a charm in each, since she had learned witchcraft from her mother. And once when the King had ridden to the hunt, she took the little shirts and went into the wood, and the ball of yarn showed her the way. The children, who saw someone in the distance, thought it was their dear father coming to see them and came jumping for joy to meet him. Then the wicked Queen threw over each of them one of the little shirts, and as soon as the shirts touched their bodies, they were changed into swans and flew away through the wood.

So the Queen went home much pleased to think she had got rid of her stepchildren, but since the maiden had not run out with her brothers the Queen knew nothing about her. The next day the King went to see his children, but he found nobody but his daughter.

"Where are your brothers?" asked the King.

"Ah, dear father," answered she, "they have gone away and have left me behind." Then she told him how from her window she had seen her brothers in the guise of swans fly away through the wood. And she showed him the feathers which they had let fall in the courtyard, and which she had picked up. The King was grieved, but he never dreamt that it was the Queen who had done this wicked deed. And as he feared lest the maiden also should be stolen away from him, he wished to take her away with him. But she was afraid of the stepmother and begged the

King to let her remain one more night in the castle in the wood.

Then she said to herself, "I must stay here no longer, but go and seek my brothers." And when night came, she ran away straight into the wood.

She went on all that night and the next day, until she could go no longer for weariness. At last she saw a rude hut, and she went in and found a room with six little beds in it. She did not dare to lie down in one, but she crept under one and lay on the hard boards and wished for night. When it was near sunset she heard a rustling sound and saw six swans come flying in at the window. They alighted on the ground and blew at one another until they had blown all their feathers off, and then they stripped off their swan skins as if they had been shirts. When the maiden looked at them and knew them for her brothers, she was very glad and crept out from under the bed. The brothers were not less glad when their sister appeared, but their joy did not last long.

"You must not stay here," they said to her. "This is a robbers' haunt, and if they were to come and find you here they would kill you."

"And cannot you defend me?" asked the little sister.

"No," answered they, "for we can only get rid of our swan skins and keep our human shape every evening for a quarter of an hour. After that we must be changed again into swans."

Their sister wept at hearing this and said, "Can nothing be done to set you free?"

"Oh no," answered they, "the work would be too hard for you. For six whole years you would be obliged never to speak or laugh, and during that time you would have to make six little shirts out of aster flowers. If you were to let fall a single word before the work was ended, all your work would be of no avail."

And just as the brothers had finished telling her this, the quarter of an hour came to an end and they changed into swans and flew out of the window.

But the maiden made up her mind to set her brothers free, even though it should cost her her life. She left the hut and went into the middle of the wood, where she climbed a tree and there passed the night. The next morning she set to work and gathered asters and began sewing them together. As for speaking, there was no one to speak to. And as for laughing, she had no mind to laugh. So she sat there and looked at nothing but her work.

When she had been going on like this for a long time, it happened that the King of that country went hunting in the wood, and some of his huntsmen came up to the tree in which the maiden sat.

They called out to her, "Who are you?" But she gave no answer.

"Come down," they cried. "We will do you no harm." But she only shook her head.

When they tormented her further with questions, she threw down to them her gold necklace, hoping they would be content with that, but they would not leave off. So she threw her sash down to them, and when that did no good she threw down her garters; and one after another everything she had on and could possible spare, until she had nothing left but her smock. But it all did no good; the huntsmen would not be put off any longer. And they climbed the tree, carried the maiden off, and brought her to the King.

The King asked, "Who are you? What were you doing in the tree?" But she answered nothing.

He spoke to her in all the languages he knew, but she remained dumb. But, since she was very beautiful, the King felt a great love rise up in his heart towards her, and casting his mantle round her, he put her before him on his horse and brought her to his castle. Then he caused rich clothing to be put upon her, and her beauty shone as bright as the morning, but no word would she utter.

He seated her by his side at table, and her modesty and gentle mien so pleased him that he said, "This maiden I choose for wife, and no other in all the world." And accordingly after a few days they were married.

But the King had a wicked mother, who was displeased with the marriage, and spoke ill of the young Queen.

"Who knows where this maid can have come from," said she, "who is not able to speak a word? She is not worthy of a king!"

After a year had passed and the Queen brought her first child into the world, the old woman carried it away, and marked the Queen's mouth with blood as she lay sleeping. Then she went to the King and declared that his wife was an eater of human flesh. The King would not believe such a thing and ordered that no one should do her any harm. And the Queen went on quietly sewing the shirts and caring for nothing else. The next time that a fine boy was born, the wicked woman used the same deceit, but the King would give no credence to her words.

He said, "She is too tender and good to do any such thing, and if she were only not dumb, and could defend herself, then her innocence would be as clear as day."

When for the third time the old woman stole away the newborn child and accused the Queen, who was unable to say a word in her own defense, the King could do nothing else but give her up to justice, and she was sentenced to suffer death by fire.

The day on which her sentence was to be carried out was the very last day of the six years during which she was neither to speak nor laugh, in order to free her dear brothers from the evil spell. The six shirts were ready, all except one which lacked the left sleeve. And when she was led to the pile of wood, she carried the six shirts on her arm. When she mounted the pile and the fire was about to be kindled, all at once she cried out aloud, for there were six swans coming flying through the air. She saw that her deliverance was near, and her heart beat for joy.

The swans came close up to her with rushing wings and stooped round her, so that she could throw the shirts over them. And when that had been done the swan skins fell off them, and her brothers stood before her in their own bodies quite safe and sound. But as one shirt wanted the left sleeve, so the youngest brother had a swan's wing instead of a left arm. They embraced and kissed each other, and the Queen went up to the King, who looked on with astonishment, and began to speak to him.

"Dearest husband," she said, "now I may dare to speak and tell you that I am innocent, and have been falsely accused." And she related to him the treachery of the old woman who had taken away the three children and hidden them. And she was reconciled to the King with great joy, and the wicked mother was bound to the stake on the pile of wood and burnt to ashes.

And the King and Queen lived many years with their six brothers in peace and joy.

The Straw, the Coal, and the Bean

Once there was a poor old woman who lived in a village. She had collected a bundle of beans and was going to cook them. So she prepared a fire on her hearth, and to make it burn up quickly she lighted it with a handful of straw. When she threw the beans into the pot, one escaped her unnoticed and slipped onto the floor, where it lay by a straw. Soon afterwards a glowing coal jumped out of the fire and joined the others.

Then the straw began and said, "Little friends, how did you come here?"

The coal answered, "I have happily escaped the fire, and if I had not done so by force of will, my death would certainly have been a most cruel one. I should have been burnt to a cinder."

The bean said, "I also have escaped so far with a whole skin. But if the old woman had put me into the pot, I should have been pitilessly boiled down to broth like my comrades."

"Would a better fate have befallen me, then?" asked the straw. "The old woman packed all my brothers into the fire and smoke. Sixty of them were all done for at once. Fortunately I slipped through her fingers."

"What are we to do now, though?" asked the coal.

"My opinion is," said the bean, "That, as we have escaped death, we must all keep together like good comrades. And so that we may run no further risks, we had better quit the country."

This proposal pleased both the others, and they set out together. Before long they came to a little stream where there was neither path nor bridge, and they did not know how to get over.

The straw at last had an idea and said, "I will throw myself over and then you can walk across upon me like a bridge."

So the straw stretched himself across from one side to the other, and the coal, which was of a fiery nature, tripped gaily over the newly built bridge. But when it got to the middle and heard the water rushing below, it was frightened and remained speechless, not daring to go any further. The straw, beginning to burn, broke in two and fell into the stream. The coal, falling with it, fizzled out in the water. The bean, who had cautiously remained on the bank, could not help laughing over the whole business, and having begun could not stop, but laughed till she split her sides. Now all would have been up with her had not, fortunately, a wandering tailor been taking a rest by the stream. As he had a sympathetic heart, he brought out a needle and thread and stitched her up again, but as he used black thread all beans have a black seam to this day.